WINTER
Magic

STRIPES PUBLISHING
An imprint of Magi Publications
1 The Coda Centre, 189 Munster Road, London SW6 6AW

A paperback original
First published in Great Britain in 2009

ISBN: 978-1-84715-107-0

WINTER
Magic

Illustrated by Alison Edgson

Stripes

CONTENTS

THE WINTER WOOD FEAST

Michael Broad

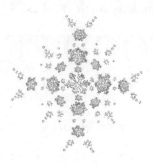

The mouse and the rabbit huddled together as they tugged their sledge through the snowdrifts, away from Winter Wood. It was the night before Christmas, a time when the woodland animals usually gathered for their festive feast, but a sudden blizzard had frozen the soil and locked away their underground stores.

"We should be singing songs around a crackling fire," sighed the young grey mouse, glancing back at their furry friends who had gathered to wave them off. "We should be eating nuts and berries and mince pies and plum puddings!"

"I know," said the brown rabbit, giving one last wave to the hopeful animals through a veil of falling snowflakes. "But we volunteered to take the sledge out to search for food, so everyone is counting on us."

The mouse and the rabbit trudged bravely up the hill to their favourite foraging ground. But when they reached the top, a thick blanket of snow covered the meadow, with white lumps and bumps where the bushes had been.

"Everything is frozen," sighed the mouse.

The rabbit nodded sadly and was wondering where they might go next when his ears suddenly twitched at a distant sound. In the still winter night he caught the merry chime of sleigh bells, and a moment later the mouse heard it.

The pair looked up to see a trail of lights sparkling in the sky.

"It's Santa Claus!" gasped the mouse, as the lights drew closer to reveal seven reindeer pulling a silver sleigh. "He's sure to bring us food for the woodland feast, all we have to do is wish."

"Santa grants wishes for human children all around the world," said the rabbit. "I don't think he has time to visit woodland animals, too."

"Oh, I'm sure he would if he knew we were hungry," said the mouse, clasping his paws together and closing his eyes tightly. "Please bring us some food, Santa Claus," he whispered, and then blinked up at the sky as the man in red soared overhead.

"He must not have heard," said the rabbit, comforting his friend as the sleigh continued across the sky, heading for the valley where the humans lived. "Though I'm sure he would have helped us if he could…"

"LOOK!" gasped the mouse, pointing upwards. As the reindeer dived into the valley, a parcel tumbled from the sleigh and landed in the snow. "Santa did hear my wish and has sent us some food!"

The mouse and the rabbit hurried across the sloping drifts, pulling the sledge behind them, until they reached the parcel. The mouse immediately tore at the wrapping paper, but when the gift was revealed he squeaked with alarm as two sleepy brown eyes stared up at him.

"Hello," said the teddy bear in the parcel. "Is it Christmas morning already?"

The mouse slowly shook his head and then looked at his friend. The rabbit was surprised, too, but quickly helped the bear to his feet. The mouse searched the wrapping paper and eventually found a shiny gold label with writing on it.

"The present wasn't for us!" gasped the mouse.

"Santa must have dropped it by accident!" gasped the rabbit.

The bear scratched his head as the animals scampered to the edge of the meadow and peered down at the small, sleeping village in the valley. Santa's sleigh had left tracks on the snowy rooftops, but he was already long gone.

"We'll have to find Sara and deliver her gift," said the rabbit.

"But what about the food?" asked the mouse, because all of the excitement and running around had made his belly rumble. "We still haven't found anything for the woodland feast."

"Christmas is a time for helping others," said the rabbit, as they made their way back to the sledge and the bear. "This teddy doesn't have a home and there's a little girl without a present for Christmas morning."

"But how will we find her?" asked the mouse.

"I have some friends who are sure to help," said the rabbit. "Magical creatures from Winter Wood, who leave their treetop homes once a year to make sure all of the children in the valley have a wonderful Christmas."

"Who are they?" asked the mouse.

"You'll see," smiled the rabbit.

The mouse and rabbit helped the teddy bear on to the sledge and pushed it to the edge of the meadow. Then they jumped up front, tipping the sledge and sending it sliding towards the village. The two animals soon forgot their hunger, laughing as they ploughed through the drifts in a shower of snowflakes. And the teddy bear laughed, too, trusting his new friends to find his home.

"WEEEEEEEEE!" they cheered as the ride picked up speed.

"EEEEEK!" gasped the mouse and the rabbit, when the sledge began to wobble.

"This is almost as fast as Santa's sleigh!" chuckled the bear, taking hold of the reins. Being the biggest, he was able to guide them over the steeper slopes, and as the sledge neared the narrow streets of the village, he planted his furry feet in the snow to bring them to a gentle stop.

"So who are your magical friends from Winter Wood?" asked the mouse, scuttling up to the nearest house, where coloured lights twinkled on the Christmas tree in the window. "Are they mice like me or rabbits like you?"

"They're not animals at all," said the rabbit, gently tapping on the windowpane.

As the mouse, bear and rabbit watched in wonder, the Christmas tree quivered and a tiny fairy fluttered down from the topmost branch. Delicate wings shimmered in the light as the fairy opened the window and smiled at the visitors.

"Can I help you?" she whispered, so as not to wake the children sleeping upstairs.

"Does a girl called Sara live here?" asked the rabbit, bringing forward the hopeful looking teddy. "Her gift got lost and we have to deliver it by morning."

"I have a boy called David and a girl called Meg, but there's no Sara here, I'm afraid," said the fairy with a concerned frown. "You could ask my sister who watches over the house next door."

"Thank you," said the rabbit. "And Merry Christmas."

"Merry Christmas," said the fairy, and closed the window.

The rabbit, mouse and bear tried the house next door, and the one next to that, and the one next to that. They kept on going until they had tapped on every bright window in every street, asking all of the tree fairies if they knew the little girl. But as each fairy listed the names of their children, none of them was called Sara.

"I don't think Sara lives in this village," sighed the mouse.

"She could live anywhere in the world," sighed the rabbit.

The mouse and rabbit looked around for the bear, but he was no longer behind them. He had been very quiet during the search for Sara so they thought he would be sad and in need of comfort. But when they followed his paw prints in the snow, they found him smiling and waving at something and he seemed very happy.

"What's he doing?" whispered the mouse, as the bear began jumping up and down.

The rabbit looked at the post office across the street. No Christmas tree could be seen through the wooden shutters, but there was a little girl in a pink nightgown in the window above. She spotted the bear and started smiling and waving back.

"Could that really be Sara?" the mouse and rabbit said together.

Suddenly the girl disappeared from the window and moments later the door burst open. The mouse and rabbit quickly hid behind the sledge as the girl ran out into the street.

"I knew Santa wouldn't forget me," said Sara, scooping the bear into her arms and hugging him tightly. "I saw him visit all the other houses, and worried that he wouldn't find our flat above the post office. But here you are, my very own bear!"

The teddy peered over the little girl's shoulder and waved a paw to say "thank you" to his friends as Sara took him inside and closed the door behind her.

The mouse and rabbit were very happy to have delivered the gift, but now they were left in the snow with a long walk home.

"We should have asked for some food for our trouble," said the mouse, as they climbed back up the steep valley slope, dragging the empty sledge behind them. "The little girl might have brought us something nice from the kitchen."

"Doing something good is reward enough," said the rabbit.

"I guess you're right," sighed the mouse, as they made their way across the meadow. "I just hope our woodland friends will understand when we return home with nothing for the feast."

It was long past midnight when the mouse and rabbit approached Winter Wood. There was no one waiting for them, and as they made their way through the winding paths, the place was quiet and still.

"Where is everyone?" asked the mouse.

The rabbit tipped his head and twitched his ears. Then he dropped the sledge, took the mouse by the paw and hurried through the trees in the direction of distant sounds. When they reached the clearing at the centre of Winter Wood, all of the animals were gathered around a large parcel.

"It arrived a short while ago!" said the deer.

"Santa dropped it from his sleigh!" added the badger.

The mouse and rabbit approached the gift, thinking Santa Claus was awfully clumsy this year. They also wondered how they would heave such a large parcel on to their sledge to take it to its real owner.

"This was tied to it!" said the owl, fluttering down with a gold label in his beak.

The rabbit took the label and read it aloud.

For the
Mouse and Rabbit
of Winter Wood

Thank you,
from Santa

"Santa did hear my wish!" gasped the mouse, leaping on to the parcel and tearing away strips of wrapping paper. The other animals all joined in and the rabbit watched with joy as they tugged and ripped to reveal a hamper filled with nuts and berries and mince pies and plum puddings, and everything needed for a wonderful feast.

ANNIE'S
CAMEL

Adèle Geras

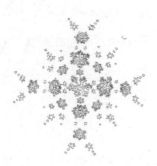

Mrs Wilson, Class Two's teacher, was explaining to the children what she wanted them to do.

"It's Christmas very soon, so could you think of something you might bring in from home which we could put into our class Nativity Scene. What sorts of things do you think we might have, children? Any ideas?"

"A Power Ranger, Miss," said Sammy.

Mrs Wilson sighed. "No, Sammy. They didn't have Power Rangers in those days."

Julie put up her hand. "Sheep, Miss. I've got a toy woolly sheep."

"That's more like it." Mrs Wilson smiled. "Sheep are good. Also goats or donkeys or even chickens, at a stretch."

"I've got a baby doll," said Parveen. "That could be the Baby Jesus."

"And I've got a doll that could be Mary," said Marie. "It's a Barbie doll, but we could dress it up in a blue dress, maybe."

"Maybe," said Mrs Wilson, though she didn't sound very sure.

"Anyway, children, you see what you can find and we'll work hard over the next few days putting our Nativity Scene together."

Annie lay in bed and wondered what she could take to school in the morning. Class Two had been working hard for days making everything look just right. Hannah had brought in a beautiful doll to be Mary and Mrs Wilson borrowed a papier mâché figure of a man from the Art Studio to be Joseph. Lots of children brought animals of one kind or another to add to the scene, but not Annie. She hadn't brought anything. Her animals were either too big (like her teddy, for instance) or not the right kind of creature (like her jungle animals and her little brother's dinosaurs). She had a baby doll, but Parveen had already been told that her doll was going to be the Baby Jesus. Mrs Wilson wouldn't need two babies.

"I'd love to be in the Nativity Scene, you know," said a snuffly voice. It sounded exactly as if it was coming from the shelf above Annie's bed.

"Who's that? Who's in my room? I'll call my mummy…"

"It's me. Camel. Don't you remember me, Annie?"

Annie stood up in her bed and peered at the shelf. Where was Camel? She felt a bit bad because what he said was quite true and she *had* forgotten all about him. Her Uncle Monty brought him back two years ago from a holiday in Tunisia and Annie hadn't liked him particularly. She'd just put Camel up on the shelf, behind some boxes of jigsaw puzzles and then she forgot all about him. He didn't do anything, that was the problem. Also, he was too small. He was made out of wood from an olive tree, Uncle Monty had told her, and she'd said "thank you", but secretly wished he'd brought her something pretty and sparkling instead.

"I didn't know you could talk," she whispered, picking Camel up between her fingers and bringing him down to stand on her bedside table in the dim light of the All-Night-Long lamp.

"I only talk when I have something to say," Camel snuffled. Annie had to lean over and put her ear right next to where he was standing because he spoke very softly. "Did you know that I come from a country quite close to the Holy Land? I would fit in perfectly in a Nativity Scene."

"Are you quite sure?" Annie hadn't ever seen a camel in a Nativity Scene. Maybe Camel just wanted to be taken to school.

"I'm as sure as I can be," Camel said. "How do you think the Three Wise Men travelled across the desert to Bethlehem? They didn't ride there on a bus, I can tell you. They didn't sail there on a boat, either. No, they came on camels. Camels are sometimes called The Ships of the Desert.

I'm sure your teacher will tell you that what I'm saying is quite true."

"Well, then, OK," Annie said. "I'll take you in to school and we'll see what Mrs Wilson thinks. Is that all right?"

"Perfect," said Camel. Annie got out of bed and took a sock out of her sock drawer.

"You don't mind being wrapped in a sock and put in my school bag, do you?" she asked.

"Not in the least."

Annie tucked Camel safely inside the sock and placed him in her school bag, which was on the chair next to her door.

"There you are, then," she said. "Sleep well. I'll see you tomorrow."

Annie got back into bed and fell asleep at once.

"Please, Miss," said Annie. "I've brought a camel. The Three Kings came to see Baby Jesus riding on camels, didn't they?"

"I'm sure they did, dear," said Mrs Wilson, coming over to look at the tiny wooden creature that Annie had pulled out of a school sock. "But your camel is a little small, isn't he? He's even smaller than Baby Jesus. That might look a bit funny. And in any case, we haven't got the Kings coming to visit the stable in this Nativity Scene."

Annie looked so disappointed that Mrs Wilson said, "Don't look so sad, Annie. You can be in charge of putting all the straw around the crib. That's a very important job and I need someone sensible to do it. All right?"

Annie nodded, but she didn't feel all right at all.

Camel spoke then, and Annie nearly dropped him. "I've had an idea."

"I don't think it will work, whatever it is," whispered Annie. "Mrs Wilson says you're smaller than the Baby Jesus. You're just not big enough and the Kings are not going to be in our Nativity anyway, so even if you were big enough, she wouldn't want you."

"I could be a toy," said Camel. "Tell her that the Baby Jesus' daddy was a carpenter and that he carved a little toy to stand at the bottom of Jesus' crib. He carved it out of wood from the tree outside the house where he and Mary lived."

"But babies like soft toys, not hard wooden ones."

"In the olden days," said Camel, "babies didn't have as many soft toys as they do these days. They had wooden dolls. Why shouldn't Baby Jesus have a wooden toy camel?"

"Annie! You're not paying attention," said Mrs Wilson. "We're nearly ready to have the straw put around the stable. The bag's on my desk. Could you bring it over here? Thank you!"

Annie went to fetch the bag and Mrs Wilson showed her how to scatter the straw around the crib and the feet of the sheep and donkeys and chickens standing around the Nativity Scene.

"You can't do that with one hand," Mrs Wilson said. "What are you holding?"

"It's my camel. He really, really wants to be in our Nativity Scene. Couldn't he be a toy? Joseph, Jesus' daddy, was a carpenter. Maybe he carved the camel out of wood from an olive tree outside his and Mary's house? Didn't babies have toys in those days? I know he's too small to be a proper camel in the scene, but couldn't he sit at the bottom of the crib for the Baby Jesus to look at when he's bored?"

Mrs Wilson laughed. "Camel wants to be in the Nativity, does he? How do you know?"

"He told me so. He can speak because he's a magic camel."

"A magic camel?" Mrs Wilson smiled. "In that case, we shouldn't leave him out, should we? Let's put him down here..."

She tucked Camel into the folds of the knitted blue blanket which Rosie had brought in to cover the Baby Jesus.

"That's lovely," said Annie. She spread the rest of the straw around the crib and made sure all the animals were standing in it tidily.

After that, Class Two went back to their seats. Everyone was busy doing sums in their workbooks and didn't notice, but Annie saw Camel lifting one of his feet and waving at her from the crib.

And was that a smile? Did camels smile? Even magic ones? Her camel could, she was quite sure, and that made her feel very happy. This year's Class Two Nativity Scene was going to be the best one ever.

CLEVER
CHARLIE

Tanya Landman

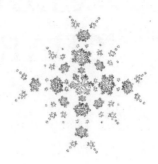

When Jessica Jones looked out of her bedroom window on Christmas morning a pony was standing in the front garden.

Jessica had always wanted a pony. She wanted one so badly that it hurt. Every night she curled into a tight ball beneath the duvet and wished and wished until her insides ached.

Jessica had riding lessons once a week. She spent six days looking forward to it, and then it would be over in what seemed like the blink of an eye.

At the top of every Christmas and birthday list she wrote, "Please, please can I have a pony." And every Christmas and birthday she would receive strangely shaped presents containing plastic, or china, or wooden ponies. The window sill in her bedroom was full of them. Once – in sheer desperation – she'd written a note to the tooth fairy, "I don't want any money. Please could I have a pony instead?"

It worked – sort of. The tooth fairy left a tiny silver pony that Jessica now wore on a chain around her neck. They were nice things to have, but plastic ponies and pretty necklaces weren't enough to fill the gaping hole in Jessica's heart. She longed to love a real live pony of her own.

But – despite all that wanting and wishing and waiting – it was still a shock when she looked out and saw the pony standing there.

Jessica's heart missed a beat. He was perfect. Absolutely perfect. A pretty dapple grey in a bright red headcollar.

Somewhere at the back of her mind Jessica knew that he wasn't *really* for her. Mum and Dad had gone through it all often enough – they couldn't afford a pony and that was that. But then… Maybe Dad had won the lottery and hadn't told her. Or maybe Father Christmas had fixed things. For a few glorious minutes Jessica allowed herself to think that a miracle had occurred – that the pony was hers. She was filled with pure joy.

Jessica tiptoed quietly downstairs – she didn't want to break the magic of the moment by waking her parents. At the front door she paused with her hand on the latch.

She wasn't sure that the beautiful creature would still be outside when she opened the door. She thought she might have imagined him. With a fierce longing she *wished* for him to be there, waiting for her. She wished for him to be *hers*.

She opened the door a fraction.

There he was. Liquid brown eyes gazing back at her as she stared through the gap. He whickered softly in greeting.

Jessica had never had such a warm welcome before. She'd heard the ponies at the riding school talking to each other when they were turned out at the end of the day – soft snuffled conversations in horse. But none of them had ever greeted *her*. Not *personally*.

She walked out in her bare feet, the grass cold between her toes.

"Hello," she whispered.

The pony lifted its nose to hers and puffed a warm breath in her face.

She'd seen horses do this, too — snorting and blowing seemed to be the horsey way of telling someone what your name was and where you were from. She blew back gently up his nostrils. Now they were properly introduced, the pony lowered his head and Jessica reached out to stroke him.

She slid her hand under his mane, feeling down the length of his warm neck, looking for the itchy place that she knew would drive him into a happy daze. No one had taught Jessica how to do it. She'd discovered for herself a long time ago that most animals have a particular spot that they love to have scratched. Jessica knew that if you found the right place on a pony, first its top lip would go all loose and floppy and then it would begin to flick and twitch. And if you carried on for long enough, the pony would eventually rest its nose on your shoulder and start to scratch you back with its velvety top lip.

They were standing there – Jessica scratching the pony's mane, the pony thoughtfully rubbing Jessica's neck and chewing the collar of her pyjamas – when Mum appeared at the open front door.

"Jessica!" she gasped. "What on earth?"

And then Dad said, "Oh Jessica."

His voice was heavy with sadness.

The spell was broken. The world crashed down around Jessica's ears. A tide of emotions washed through her, draining out through her bare feet and sinking into the lawn. The tone of their voices had said it all. The pony *wasn't* a surprise present. Dad *hadn't* won the lottery. Father Christmas hadn't fixed things. The pony wasn't *hers*. He was an escapee. A runaway.

And he would have to go back.

Some other girl would be missing him right now ... looking frantically in his field ... calling the police...

They let her stay with the pony while Dad made some phone calls. In no time at all he was back.

"He belongs to a Mrs Cox," Dad said gently. "He's come a long way. She lives over at the Old School House. That big place just off the green."

Jessica swallowed. "Is she coming to collect him?"

"No..." said Dad uncertainly. "I said you'd take him back. Was that OK?"

Dad held the pony while Jessica went to get dressed. She tugged on her old jeans and hand-me-down boots, and then pulled her scruffy riding hat out from under the bed.

"You're never going to *ride* him?" asked Mum anxiously, as Jessica came back out into the garden. "You haven't got a saddle or anything."

"He's got a headcollar on," answered Jessica. "We can tie on some rope for reins."

"But…" Mum stared at the pony on the lawn. "Is he *safe?*"

Jessica looked into his beautiful brown eyes. That was the other thing Jessica knew about horses. You could tell a lot about them by the expression in their eyes. *His* eyes were generous. *His* eyes were kind. *His* eyes invited Jessica to trust him.

"Yes," Jessica said with total confidence. "He's safe."

It was a dream of a ride.

From the moment Jessica scrambled on to the pony's back and took up the pair of Dad's second-best ties that they had used for reins, Jessica knew that this pony was as different from the riding school ones as it was possible for any creature to be.

Jessica always felt a bit guilty about the way the riding school ponies trudged tiredly around the outdoor school. She knew perfectly well that they'd rather be grazing quietly in the field than carrying her round and round in endless circles. But this pony stepped out briskly, in an eager walk, his ears flicking backwards and forwards as he took everything in. He carried her as if they were embarking on the most exciting journey in the world. Together. As equals. Partners. Friends. It was thrilling – a totally new experience. Jessica suddenly felt that on this pony she could do anything.

This pony was listening, responding to anything and everything Jessica did. And it wasn't so much her hands or legs or voice he was answering to, Jessica realized with a jolt of surprised delight, he was responding to her *thoughts*. She had only to spot a stretch of straight road that would be good for a trot, and he would go forward with a smooth, light, floating action that was a delight, even bareback. Every time they came to a grass verge, he flicked an ear back towards her, seeming to ask, "Shall we?" Jessica would think, "Yes!" and he would lift into a fluid canter.

Suddenly those lessons where she had bounced up and down in the saddle of a reluctant pony, unable to keep her seat, with her instructor yelling, "Supple! Keep your back supple!" all fell into place. She flexed her spine, absorbing the pony's movement in the small of her back, and relaxed into perfect harmony with him. She sat easily, comfortably, with her seat as secure as if her bottom had been superglued to his back.

It was over too quickly. Dad had followed some way behind her on his bike, unwilling to interrupt the ride by talking to her. In less than an hour they were within sight of the Old School House. Jessica had one last glorious gallop across the village green, leaning forward over the pony's neck, the wind whipping into her face, sucking the

breath out of her. Then they were there —
outside a pair of wrought iron gates.
Somewhere inside that big house was a girl
who could ride him every day. Jessica couldn't
bear it. She slid to the ground, rested her face
against his cheek and whispered, "It's not fair!
It's not fair! It's not *fair!*"

She only knew that someone had come
out of the house when she heard Dad
behind her.

"Hello," he called. "Mrs Cox, is it?"

"Yes. Happy Christmas," said a woman's
voice. "It's Mr Jones, isn't it? And Jessica?
Thank you so much for bringing him back."

Jessica looked up. The woman was older
than Dad, Jessica reckoned, dressed in
shabby old jeans and a comfy cardigan.

"I was so worried," she told Jessica. "I nearly had heart failure when I looked out and saw he wasn't there. It's the second time this week." She turned to the pony. "He's bored, poor old boy. You're feeling a bit neglected, aren't you?"

The sheer injustice of it stabbed Jessica. Some lucky girl had a pony as good as this and she *neglected* him? Whoever she was, she didn't deserve him. Mrs Cox was looking at Jessica. "You ride very well. I saw you coming across the green. Have you got your own pony, Jessica?" she asked.

Jessica shook her head. There was a lump in her throat that prevented her from speaking.

Dad stepped in. "No… She gets a lesson once a week up at the riding school. She'd love one of her own, of course, but … well … it's just not possible…"

"What a pity," said Mrs Cox. "That's hard on someone who rides as well as Jessica."

"What's his name?" asked Jessica quietly. She suddenly wanted to say goodbye to the pony properly.

"Charlie," answered Mrs Cox. "He's my daughter's really."

"So where is she?" demanded Jessica. She wanted to see the girl who would neglect a pony like Charlie. The girl who wouldn't even come out of the house to see that he'd got safely home.

Mrs Cox seemed to know what Jessica was thinking. "Actually, Jessica, Lynne's on a gap year at the moment. She's teaching in Africa. That's why he's feeling lonely." Mrs Cox sighed. "It's so difficult to know quite what to do with him. We can't *sell* him — he's such a family pet. None of us could *bear* to part with him." She looked at Jessica. "But you know he could do with *someone* to take him out now and again…"

The sentence hung in the air. Jessica didn't dare say anything. Her heart was pounding uncontrollably against her ribs. Hope flickered like a bright flame just behind her eyes. And at the same time, fear rose in her throat — the fear that she hadn't heard right, the fear that what she was hoping for couldn't possibly happen. It was just too good to be true.

"Would *you* like to, Jessica?" asked Mrs Cox. "Charlie does seem to have taken rather a fancy to you. *Could* you take him out sometimes? I mean, would you have *time*?"

It was all too much. It was too wonderful to take in.

Jessica buried her face in Charlie's mane and burst into tears.

"Oh dear," said Mrs Cox, confused. "I'm sorry," she said to Dad. "I didn't mean to upset her."

Dad's voice wobbled as a huge grin broke across his face. "Jessica's *happy*. It's a dream come true for her. Your big problem will be keeping her away! You've made her day. Best Christmas surprise she's ever had."

"Really?" said Mrs Cox. "How funny!"

"Why?"

"Because that's his name," she said, stroking the pony's face. "His proper name. The one the breeder gave him. Stupid great long show name. We always call him Charlie. But his real name's 'Clever Charlie's Christmas Surprise'."

THE MOUSE'S TALE

Penny Dolan

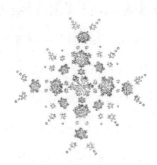

What did that cat want as it sneaked into our church with snow on its fur and hunger in its whiskers? What did it want as it crept round the tall Christmas tree? Even I, a small mouse, knew what that cat wanted. That cat wanted mice for its dinner!

Most of the time, nobody notices us church mice. We live behind the wooden panelling. We sleep in nests made of ribbons and feathers from ladies' bonnets.

We eat crumbs that fall from children's pockets, and wax candle stubs, and cheese rinds from the cleaner's supper. We enjoy living here in peace and quiet.

But we do like to hear our bells calling people to sing, especially at Christmas. Our choir is the best choir in the city, and that is because Father Franz, the music-master, loves to make music.

However, if Father Franz hadn't been sitting at the organ that evening, that cat might have gone away. As it was, the cat came right in, and mewed and nuzzled at his knees.

"Poor thing," said Father Franz, absent-mindedly. "You shouldn't be out on such a wintry night. Maybe you should stay here till morning?"

What? Stay here? I couldn't believe my ears! The church was our home! Perhaps the cat would refuse? No! The wretched thing jumped up on to the bench beside him, and curled itself up, purring.

Father Franz was at work composing a new carol. Note by note, he picked out the new tune on the keyboard. Then he wrote it down on paper.

"It's still not right," he muttered, frowning. "I don't think this tune matches Father Josef's words."

Time was running out for music making.

The new carol was needed for tomorrow's Christmas celebrations. Father Franz pumped away at the bellows, filling the organ with air again, so the organ pipes would sing aloud.

I must add that I was not just watching Father Franz. I was watching the delicious fruit cake that stood on a pretty plate at his side. Frau Schmidt, the baker's wife, had brought him the cake as a Christmas gift. He was already nibbling away at the spicy slices.

"No time for a meal tonight," he muttered to himself as he worked.

Oh dear! That cake was disappearing quickly. Would any of it be left for us? And now, with that cat sitting there, would we even be able to reach it?

At long last, Father Franz wrote his final notes and put down his pen. He played his new tune through once more, and then stood up, yawning.

"Perhaps it will sound better tomorrow," he said, sighing. "The choir can practise it properly in the morning. Now I need my bed."

"Miaow!" said the cat. It stretched lazily, and then curled up on the warm cushion that Father Franz had just left.

"Sleep comfortably, cat," said Father Franz. He spread a cloth over the remains of the cake and left, taking a lantern to guide him through the dark, snowy streets.

Within moments, I heard the cat jump down, and start prowling about on its four soft paws. I scurried back to the mouse hole to warn my brothers and sisters to stay hidden. Though the cat searched, it didn't see a single mouse. At last, it settled back down on Father Franz's cushion and closed its eyes tightly.

By now, we were very hungry for some of that cake. I led the way across the polished floor, with the boldest mice following behind me. Sniff, sniff! The sweet cake scent lured us towards that pretty plate.

Then a shadow moved, a shadow pounced.

"Quick!" I squeaked. "It's the cat!"

We scrambled beneath the organ, and squeezed up through a tiny crack. We were safe inside the wooden case. Though the cat stretched out her long paws, she could not touch us, but nor could we escape.

Oh dear! We could see that cake, we could smell that cake, but we couldn't taste one crumb of it. Our tummies grumbled with hunger. All there was inside the organ was dry dust and cobwebs. Then I sniffed harder and found an interesting scent: something edible was close by. What was it? Aha!

The organ's air bag was made from good chewy leather. Surely a bite or two would

not matter much? Or ten? Or twenty?

We nibbled and nibbled. Though the leather wasn't cake, it was much better than starving.

We made small holes in the air bag, of course, but how could we help that happening? Once we started gnawing, it was impossible to stop. Finally, with our tummies full, we snuggled up safely inside the organ.

Meanwhile, angry at our escape, the cat pounced furiously on Father Franz's favourite cushion, sending the feathers flying around the church like snowflakes. We watched until we grew sleepy...

Suddenly, it was morning. The choir had come for their rehearsal. I heard them stamping the snow off their shoes, while Father Franz's heavy steps came closer to our hiding place. Behind him came Frau Schmidt with her clattering clogs.

"What's happened here? There's feathers all over the place," said Frau Schmidt, nearly dropping her basket of goodies, "and your comfy cushion's ruined!"

Father Franz sank down on the hard wooden bench. "It must have been the cat I let shelter here last night. Just wait till I see that animal!" Then he shook his head. "Never mind. We're here to work, aren't we? Choir, here's the new tune I've written for you."

While he hummed his melody, the choir listened.

"We haven't got very long to practise," one of the singers said, anxiously.

"Yes, it is a bit complicated," agreed another.

"The music's just too grand for the words," said Frau Schmidt, with a shrug. "The song needs a simpler tune."

"Let me play my tune properly," said Father Franz, sitting down at the organ. He stretched his fingers towards the keyboard, and began.

Strangely, though the bellows breathed in and out, and his feet played the pedals, the sound was not at all musical. The organ sounded as if it was coughing and wheezing, and lots of notes were out of tune.

Inside the organ, we mice sat trembling on a ledge. We had ruined his instrument.

"Whatever's wrong with it?" Father Franz bent down and peered inside. "Oh no! There's a hole in the air bag. Whatever am I going to do?" he cried.

Father Franz struck the organ so hard that I overbalanced and tumbled right out at his feet. He blinked in astonishment.

"Meow!" screeched the cat, darting out from its hiding place.

Did I run! I ran across that floor so fast that I could hardly see where I was going. I ran between shoes and boots, under skirts and petticoats, around candlesticks and along benches. I scrambled up a carved screen and back down the other side, and that cat raced up and down after me.

With one last spurt, I reached the safety of the old music cupboard, and slipped through a narrow gap between the doors. The cat leaped after me so fast that it crashed straight into the cupboard.

Both doors shot open, and out fell piles of song books, recorders and tambourines. What a noise everything made! I scampered to a safer place.

Frau Schmidt grabbed the cat, and held it in her lap. "Sshhh!" she said, stroking it until it was calm.

"Wretched cat!" said Father Franz, putting things back on the shelves. All at once he saw his guitar tucked away in a corner. He lifted down the instrument tenderly.

"Perhaps my guitar would be the right thing for our carol?" he said, smiling as he plucked the strings. Then he paused. "Wait! I think I have an idea for a new tune."

He played a simple melody. It was not grand or proud, but sweet and gentle. The choir nodded.

"What do you think?" Father Franz asked.

"I think those words and music would sound quite magical," said Frau Schmidt. "Let us give it a try."

As the choir sang the new carol, the beautiful sound echoed through the church.

"Silent Night, Holy Night
All is calm, all is bright..."

Father Josef crept quietly through the door, and stood listening. "What a lovely Christmas song," he said.

"It makes me think of candles shining from windows at night," said one singer.

"It makes me think of angels watching from the starry sky," said another.

"It makes me think of my children sleeping peacefully in their beds," said a woman.

"And the baby sleeping in the stable at Bethlehem," added another.

"This song will make me think about that little mouse who helped me find my guitar," said Father Franz, smiling.

"And that naughty cat who chased him?" added Frau Schmidt, and everyone laughed.

Then Father Josef looked solemn. He clapped his hands for silence. "Friends, you must sing Silent Night at all our Christmas services," he said, "because that carol reminds me of peace and happiness. Well done, Father Franz!"

That is exactly what happened. While candles shone brightly, the choir sang the words of the new carol:

"Silent Night, Holy Night,
All is calm, all is bright."

Everyone went home from church singing Father Josef's words and humming

Father Franz's lovely new tune. Some people took the song and sang it in other places and other lands. Father Franz's song became a famous Christmas carol called *Silent Night* – and you may even have heard it!

Of course, there was more to the story of that Christmas.

Frau Schmidt, with the cat cuddled on her lap, spoke up. "Poor thing. It's too cold to shoo this creature out on to the street. I'll take it to share my kitchen fire." Emptying her basket, she put the cat carefully inside, and toddled off home, leaving several mince pies behind her.

When everything was silent once again, we came creeping out from our hiding places. What with the sweet pies and the leftover cake, we mice had a most magical Christmas feast ready and waiting.

SNOW SWAN

Julia Green

The wounded swan flew in with the storm.

Mara found her when she went out before school, to let the hens out of their house, like she did every morning. Because it was the middle of winter, it was still dark. Snow lay on the grass, a fine white layer, shining in the half-light. And something else was there, huddled in the middle of the field.

Mara opened the gate and went through into the field, the bucket of feed bumping against her legs. At first she thought it was a goose, but then she saw the beautiful long neck, the webbed feet, and the black beak with a patch of yellow, and she knew it was a swan. A special kind of wild swan – not the same as the tame ones that swam on the lake in the park near the school.

The swan cried out, a mournful sound, *whoop-a*, when it saw Mara. It tried to fly away, but it couldn't, because of its wounded wing.

Mara called out, softly, so as not to frighten it. "Don't be scared, swan!" she said. "I'm not going to hurt you. Here – have some food!" She threw a handful of chicken food from the bucket, on to the snowy grass and left the swan to eat it.

Mara's boots made neat prints in the snow. She went to the hen house and opened the little door, hooking it up with the string on the nail, so that the hens could come out to peck and scratch in the field. She filled the hopper with pellets, and she broke the ice on the water trough, so the hens could drink.

There was no point in checking for eggs. In the deep winter, the hens stopped laying. They would start again when the mornings got lighter, when spring came.

The hens were warm, feathers fluffed up, huddled up close together on their perch in the hen house. They peered at Mara with their beady eyes, as if to say, "It's too early to get up! It's too cold today!" They made funny noises in their throats, a contented, crooning sound, as if they were talking to each other.

"Please yourselves!" Mara said. She trudged back across the field, closing the gate behind her and fastening the latch, so the fox could not get in. Foxes were clever. They could push open a gate, or wriggle through the smallest tear in the wire fence.

Mara forgot about the swan until later, after school, when she and Mum stopped off at the library on the way home. She found a book about swans and she looked at the pictures. The swan in the field was a Whooper swan, she decided, with its black and yellow beak and the strange cry, "*Whoopa, whoopa.*" Usually the swans flew together, in big flocks. It must have been blown off course on its long winter flight from Iceland. It had got separated from its family, and had injured its wing.

The swan was still there when Mara went to shut the hens up safe for the night. It stared at her, and again tried to fly, but couldn't. "You're safe here," Mara told the swan. "The foxes can't get you in this field. Stay and rest, until your wing is better."

When she told Dad about the swan, at supper-time, he told her how all swans used to belong to the King or Queen, and how swan meat was thought to be the finest meat of all. "The wild swan would make a delicious roast dinner, for Christmas!" he said.

Mum was cross with him. "Don't tease Mara!" she said.

Mum said that a long time ago, some people thought wilds swans were messengers, or bringers of good luck. Some people thought wild swans were angels.

Mum smiled at Mara. "Perhaps your swan has a message for you," she said.

The swan got used to seeing Mara every morning and every afternoon. The cold easterly wind kept blowing, day after day, bringing more snow. The snow stayed, and so did the swan. Now, when Mara came to the gate with the bucket, the swan didn't try to fly or run – it took a step closer. Mara called her Snow Swan, because she had arrived with the snow.

Now she realized the swan wasn't going to fly away, Mara went to the barn, and found a sack of hay and an old wooden crate. She wanted to make a warm place for the snow swan to shelter in, out of the bitter wind. But the swan stayed out on the field, as if she was too afraid to go into the shelter. She plumped up her soft, white feathers to keep herself warm. She tucked her head under her good wing.

Little by little, the swan became friends with Mara.

Mara was very happy to be friends with a swan, but sometimes she felt worried, too. Not all humans could be trusted to be gentle with a wild bird. She had seen older children chasing the birds in the park, and throwing rubbish at the swans nesting on the canal. People could be cruel, sometimes. She was afraid that if someone else found out about her swan, they might try and hurt it.

The first day of the Christmas holidays, Mara slept longer than on a school day, so it was later than usual when she went out to feed the hens. Snow Swan was waiting for her, close by the gate. She stretched her long neck towards the bucket, as if she was hungry and impatient for food. Mara dipped her gloved hand into the bucket, and held out the palmful of pellets. She held her breath.

The swan looked right at her, and then took the food carefully from her hand.

Mara let out her breath with a sigh. Her heart fluttered with excitement. The swan trusted her. It felt magical to be so close to a wild creature.

The hens clucked and crooned from inside their house, eager to be fed and let out. They pushed through the little door and crowded round Mara. They scratched at the ice on the field to get at the grass beneath.

The swan moved away, keeping itself separate from the tame birds. Now that its wing had healed completely, Mara thought, there was nothing to stop it flying off.

Each morning and evening for five more days, Mara went to the field half-expecting Snow Swan to have flown. But still the swan stayed, getting braver each day. She took corn and chicken feed right out of Mara's hand. Even though she was big and strong, now, with a hard beak and powerful wings, she was gentle and trusting of Mara. Only, she would never let Mara get quite close enough to touch her soft feathers.

Christmas Eve, Mara took the hens a special bowl of warm mash in the morning, and extra corn for Snow Swan. She helped Mum decorate the Christmas tree, and then she went to town in the car with Dad, to help him do his last-minute shopping for presents.

Mara was excited. She loved Christmas! She loved the presents and the fairy lights. Best of all, her grown-up brothers would arrive tomorrow, in time for the big dinner that everyone would help cook. Granny and

Grandpa would come, too. Mara loved it when they were all together, one big family.

As soon as Mara got back from town, she went to shut the hens up safe for the night. She looked up at the blue-black sky. The moon was rising, silver bright, above the dark line of the hill. One star was already shining, hanging low in the sky, just like on a Christmas card.

Snow Swan was waiting for her at the gate. The swan spread wide her beautiful wings, and stretched out her elegant neck. "*Whoopa, whoopa,*" the swan called.

Mara knew in an instant that she was saying goodbye. She put down the bucket. Without thinking, she put her arms right round the swan. The soft feathers brushed her face. She felt the swan's warm beating heart beneath her hands, and the strength of her wings. "Go well, be free, be safe, Snow Swan," Mara whispered.

When she shut the gate and went back to the warm house, Mara had tears in her eyes.

Mara woke early on Christmas morning. It was dark; the house was silent and very still. Something had changed.

Mara went to the window, and drew back the curtains. She opened the window just a little. She heard the drip, drip sound of snow beginning to melt, trickling down from the roof.

Mara knew now what was different – the cold, easterly wind had dropped. Soon all the snow would be gone. She sat at the window, and watched until the darkness began to fade, and the first streaks of pink came in the sky above the hill. And as she sat there in the dawn, she heard another sound – the steady, rhythmic beating of wings, over the house and fading into the distance.

Snow Swan had flown.

Mara imagined her long flight, all the way back north to join the rest of the flock. The huge family of swans would have missed her. When she thought about her swan like that, going back where she belonged, Mara didn't feel so sad any more. She'd never forget her, and the magic moment when she held a wild swan in her arms. But you can't keep a wild swan, like you keep chickens or cats. Not for ever. Sometimes you have to let things go.

Mara climbed back into bed. Now it was beginning to get light, she could see the stocking on the end of her bed, stuffed with little parcels all wrapped up in blue paper with gold stars. Yes! It was Christmas Day at last!

Mara picked up the Christmas stocking, and ran down the landing to join her own family.

THE
CHRISTMAS
CAT

Holly Webb

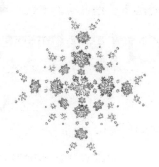

"Do we have to put this one up, Mum? It's really tatty." Lily held out a little furry ornament shaped like a kitten. It *was* tatty. It'd had whiskers once, but they were long gone, and the tip of its tail was missing, too. The pink bow round its neck was grubby and frayed.

"Oh, we can't not have Tiggy!" Mum exclaimed, taking the little ball of greyish fur and looking down at it lovingly.

"You made this for me, don't you remember? You and your dad made him together, from one of those sewing kits, when you were about, ohh, five? You were so proud of him, and you named him Tiggy."

Lily sighed loudly, but she was smiling. "OK, OK. But please can we put him round the back? Now we've got all these new glittery decorations, he doesn't really fit in."

Mum reached up and hung Tiggy the kitten on the tree, over to one side out of the way, with a silver glitter snowflake right in front of him. You wouldn't have seen him at all, if you didn't know he was there.

Lily went to bed early on Christmas Eve, much earlier than usual. She wanted it to be Christmas as soon as possible, even though it was going to be a strange one. For the first time, she wouldn't have her dad with her for Christmas Day. He was stuck in Scotland, where he'd had to go for a work trip. He should have been back yesterday, in plenty of time for Christmas, but the heavy snow had closed the airport.

Dad had been really upset when he phoned. "I'm sorry, Lily. I've tried the station, but none of the trains are running either. They said maybe on Boxing Day. I can't believe I won't be there to spend Christmas morning with you and your mum."

Lily couldn't believe it either. It seemed worse because she had been so happy about the snow! She loved snow, and she'd gone out with all the other children from her street, and they'd had a snowball fight, and made a snowman – it was still there, on her front lawn. But then that same snow had stopped her having Christmas with Dad.

Perhaps it was because she had gone to bed so early that she woke up early too. Her bedroom was still totally dark, and her alarm clock said it was only half-past five. Half-past five! Mum would be really grumpy if Lily went and woke her up now.

She wriggled one foot further down under her duvet and poked experimentally at the end of her bed. Yes! Her stocking was definitely full. She turned on her bedside light to have a look. Mum wouldn't mind her unwrapping a few of the presents. She'd save a couple to open with her later.

Her stocking was full of fun things – a new purse, some sweets, some really cute new slippers, and a couple of books. She could nibble a bit of chocolate reindeer and read for a bit – but she just didn't feel like it. Lily sniffed. It felt really wrong for it to be just her and Mum at Christmas. Why did Dad have to go and get himself stuck in the snow?

Suddenly Lily climbed out of bed, slipped her feet into her new slippers, and pulled on her fleece. She wasn't going to lie there and be miserable, she was going downstairs. She could get some juice or something, curl up on the sofa for a bit. She crept down the stairs, and sneaked into the living room. It was dark down here too, and cold. Lily turned on the Christmas tree lights, and watched them twinkle, shining on all the beautifully wrapped presents underneath. She didn't feel any more cheerful, and the tree looked spooky in the greyish morning half-light.

Lily sighed, and then something strange caught her eye – what looked like a spider's web on the Christmas tree. She reached up to pull it away, and then realized that, of course, it was Tiggy, that scruffy little ornament she and Dad had made.

Lily took him down carefully, and curled up on the sofa. She'd pretended to Mum that she didn't really remember making him, but of course she did. And she'd have been upset if Mum hadn't put him up, too.

Lily had always been into crafty things, even then, and Gran had given her the kit so she could make something for Christmas. Lily stroked Tiggy's balding head, and smiled, remembering her and Dad sitting at the kitchen table, Dad patiently threading the big plastic sewing needle for her again and again.

She had talked all the way through, about how she wished Tiggy was a real cat, grey, with brownish stripes and bright green eyes. The eyes in the kit were shiny green beads that you had to sew on, and amazingly enough, Tiggy still had both of them. Lily had told Dad all about Tiggy's favourite food – tuna sandwiches, just like her, and how he'd sleep on the end of her bed at night. Dad had laughed, and said that a real cat wouldn't let her dress him in a pink bow like that one.

Lily stared down at Tiggy's grey fur sadly. She'd always wanted a cat. But every time she asked, Mum and Dad said, "When you're older". Looking down at the big lopsided stitches that held Tiggy's green glass eyes on, Lily felt her own eyes sting, and a tear ran down the side of her nose, closely followed by another and another. Some of them soaked into Tiggy's stripy fur fabric. "Sorry," Lily muttered, stroking them away. He was nice to stroke, even if he was tatty.

Afterwards, Lily was never sure exactly when Tiggy changed. She wasn't really concentrating, just stroking the tiny cat without thinking about it. Until she wasn't stroking a furry ornament, but a great big stripy tabby cat, stretched out blissfully across her whole lap and falling off both sides. He only had two-thirds of a tail – just like the little ornament.

Lily stopped stroking him in shock, and the cat half-rolled over in a lazy way, and waved a fat stripy paw at her. *"Prrp?"* he asked, politely but clearly telling her to get back to stroking, please. Lily obediently ran her hand down his back, noticing that he was one of those gorgeous tabbies with a furry line down his spine and masses of thin stripes, like fishbones.

She gave a little giggle, wondering if he'd like a tuna sandwich, and the cat leaped off her knee, purring loudly, and looked eagerly towards the kitchen.

Almost sure now that she must be dreaming, Lily followed the cat to the fridge. She found half a tin of tuna and dolloped it generously on to a couple of slices of bread. The cat sat at her feet and mewed hungrily. Lily cut the sandwich in half and put it on two plates, which she placed on the kitchen table.

The cat immediately jumped on to a chair, and stared at her expectantly. Oh well. Mum would say it was unhygienic, but this was only a dream, so it didn't matter. Lily and Tiggy ate their sandwiches – Tiggy licked the plate, but Lily didn't – and then he stepped delicately on to Lily's lap.

Lily yawned. It was only six o'clock. She stood up, her arms full of slightly fishy-smelling cat, and padded back to the sofa, curling up against the cushions. The cat walked round her lap about seventeen times, and finally settled himself in a tight, neat ball, head and tail tucked in. Then they both fell asleep.

Lily's mum woke her up two hours later, laughing.

"What are you like, Lily! A tuna sandwich for breakfast, on Christmas Day! We'd bought those yummy chocolate croissants, don't you remember? Why didn't you wake me up?" She sat down on the sofa next to her and gave her a hug. "Happy Christmas, Lily. We'd better wait a while to ring Dad, I bet he'll still be asleep."

Lily blinked up at her, feeling dazed. Where was the cat? Oh – of course. It had been a dream. Her eyes filled suddenly with tears again, and she looked down at her empty lap miserably.

Mum peered at Lily's top, looking surprised. "Lily, what have you got all over your fleece? It looks like cat hair. Have you been playing with that cat next door?" She brushed at the front of Lily's top.

But the cat next door was black and white, and these hairs were silver-brown tabby. Lily looked up at the Christmas tree, and Tiggy was back up there. But he wasn't tucked away at the back any more. He was hanging right in the middle, where everyone could see him, and he didn't look quite as tatty as before. He looked like a very contented tabby cat, full of tuna fish.

PATRICK THE PIRATE PIG

Karen Wallace

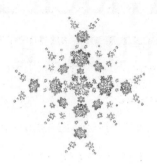

It all began when Patrick the pig found an old book about pirates in the compost heap behind the farmyard. Patrick liked to think the book had magically fallen out of the sky and landed where only he would find it. But his mother, Mrs Pig, said that was a bit silly because paper was good for compost heaps and since the book had lots of torn pages, the farmer's wife must have thrown it away on purpose. But Patrick wasn't listening.

He still thought the book was especially for him. And, besides, not all the pages were torn and some of them had amazing pictures of pirates.

Soon Patrick learned that all pirates wore battered three-cornered hats, grubby black jackets with gold braid, baggy trousers, saggy leather boots and, of course, a black eyepatch. He was particularly pleased to find out about the black eyepatch because even though Patrick was a pink pig, he had a small black patch on his shoulder.

The two pictures that Patrick liked best were of a pirate ship with a skull and crossbones flag flying from the very top of the mast and one of a pirate called Captain

Cutlass standing beside a treasure chest full of gold. Captain Cutlass had a black patch over one eye, a parrot on his shoulder and a long curved sword tucked into his belt.

Patrick liked the way the gold glittered in the picture and Captain Cutlass's eye gleamed. Sometimes, when the sun was going down and it was getting too dark in the pigpen to see, Patrick was sure Captain Cutlass's eye gleamed like a real eye and the gold glittered like real gold.

As summer turned into winter, Patrick became more and more determined to be a pirate. And little by little, he began to look like one. He found a pair of ragged trousers under a pile of hay and a three-cornered hat that had blown off a scarecrow. He made his own curved sword from a bendy stick and tied a patch of black plastic over one eye.

"Yo! Ho! Ho!" cried Patrick. He danced a little dance when the first snowflakes began to fall and waved his stick in the air. "I'm Patrick the Pirate Pig!"

One morning, a few days before Christmas, Mrs Pig took Patrick to the meadow on his own. "It's about time you stopped trying to be a pirate," she said, gently. She sighed a huge sigh, which shook the snow from a nearby bush. "I'm sorry, dear. A pig can't be a pirate and that's that."

"No, it's not," said Patrick, twitching his snout. "I can be anything I want in my head." Sometimes his mother just didn't understand. Besides, now that it was almost Christmas, Patrick had a secret plan. He was going to ask Father Christmas for a pirate ship that was small enough to float in the river at the bottom of the field. Then he could go off and have adventures just like Captain Cutlass.

"So what are you going to ask Father Christmas for?" asked Mrs Pig brightly, as if she wanted to change the subject. "How about a sack of carrots or a nice bucket of swill?"

Patrick crossed his back trotters so his mother couldn't see he was telling a fib. "I don't know yet," he said. "But I'm sure I'll think of something."

Mrs Pig smiled and nuzzled his ear. "Of course you will, darling," she said. "And it will be exactly right."

Soon it was Christmas Eve and all the other animals in the farmyard began to talk about the presents they had asked Father Christmas for.

"I'm going to get a big thick blanket and

a ton of nuts," said the horse, who was already a bit tubby and always wore two blankets even in the summer.

"I'm going to get an enormous bicycle horn so I can make a *really* loud noise in the morning," said the cockerel. He crowed with laughter. "That'll wake you all up, whether you like it or not."

The fat black cat opened one eye and yawned. "Maybe some of us don't want to wake up when it's still dark," she said in a sleepy voice.

"I don't care," crowed the cockerel. "Everyone knows I'm the most important animal in the farmyard."

Then the animals forgot about Christmas and began the same argument they had every day of the year.

"No you're not," said the cow. "I'm the most important and the farmer likes me best."

"Rubbish," said the dog. "I'm the farmer's best friend. I'm the most important."

Squawk! Moo! Meow! Baa! Bark! Bleat! Cock-a-doodle-doo!

All the animals began to shout at the same time.

Me! Me! I'm the most important animal in the farmyard!

The only one who didn't join in was Henrietta the hen. She didn't like arguing.

At that moment, Patrick walked through the gate dressed in pirate trousers and a three-cornered hat. He had a black patch over one eye and a wooden sword tucked into his belt. "Happy Christmas Eve, everyone," he shouted.

There was complete silence in the farmyard. You could have heard a mouse squeak. All the animals stared at Patrick.

Then one by one they began to laugh.

The cockerel threw back his head and went *cock-a-doodle-doo*! "A pig can't be a pirate!" he crowed. Then he began to sing a mean song. "Patrick can't be a pirate! Patrick can't be a pirate." And all the animals joined in, too.

Poor Patrick! He was so sad he ran away and locked himself in his pigpen.

Mrs Pig hurried after him. She sighed a

huge sigh that nearly blew down the door. "Remember what I said? A pig can't be a pirate. Why didn't you believe me?"

"I *can* be a pirate," cried Patrick. "I *know* I can!"

But Mrs Pig only shook her head and went away.

A little while later, Henrietta the hen tapped on the door. "Don't listen to those silly animals," she said. "You can be anything you want."

Patrick jumped up and opened the door to let her in. "Do you really think so?"

"Of course I do," said Henrietta. "You see, I've always wanted to be a pirate's parrot!" She cocked her head. "Listen to this!"

Henrietta jumped on to Patrick's shoulder and squawked, "Pretty Polly! Pretty Polly!"

Patrick was amazed. She sounded just like a real pirate's parrot!

"If I ever get my own pirate ship," said Patrick, "would you come with me?"

"Of course I would," replied Henrietta. "And guess what?"

"What?" asked Patrick.

"I've asked Father Christmas for some real parrot feathers of my own!"

That night snowflakes turned the farmyard white. When Patrick was sure all the other animals were asleep, he crept outside and wrote a letter to Father Christmas in the hard crispy snow.

There was a full moon and his letter seemed to sparkle in the bright silvery light.

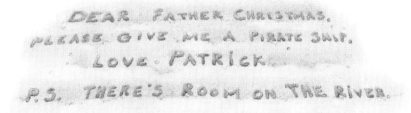

DEAR FATHER CHRISTMAS,
PLEASE GIVE ME A PIRATE SHIP.
LOVE PATRICK.
P.S. THERE'S ROOM ON THE RIVER.

The next morning, the first sound everyone heard was a *root-a-toot-too* of a horn mixed with a *cock-a-doodle-doo*!

Patrick's heart banged in his chest! Henrietta had told him that the cockerel had asked for a bicycle horn for Christmas. Maybe now he would get his ship! He poked his head out of his pigpen and looked around nervously. Snow had fallen overnight and the farmyard was white. What if snow had fallen on his letter?

"Happy Christmas, darling!" said Mrs Pig. She handed him a big bag of carrots and apples. "Did Father Christmas get you what you wanted?"

Patrick swallowed hard. All the other animals had got what they asked for. He held back a sob as he climbed on top of his pigpen and looked down at the river. There was no sign of a ship, or a sail or a flag anywhere.

Then Patrick saw something huge and white with a mast sticking out of the top.

"Yippee!" he cried and rushed down to the river. "Father Christmas read my letter!"

All the animals ran after him. Mrs Pig was so astonished she snorted like a steam train and her breath knocked the snow off a perfect pirate ship!

"Pieces of eight!" squawked Henrietta. "That's the place for me!" And she spread her new bright blue and orange wings and flew on to the deck.

Patrick was so amazed he thought his eyes would pop out of his head. It was the best Christmas present ever!

All the animals cheered as Patrick kissed his mother goodbye.

"Look after yourself," said Mrs Pig. "Don't forget your old mum." Then she gave him a Christmas pudding. "Pretend it's a ship's biscuit," she whispered.

Patrick just had time to wave to Mrs Pig before the sails filled with wind and the ship began to move. "I'll send you a postcard," he cried. "Promise!"

The ship followed a bend in the river and suddenly Patrick and Henrietta smelled salt in the air. Soon they would be sailing out to sea in search of pirate gold.

"Happy Christmas, Cap'n," squawked Henrietta. She spread her new blue and orange wings. "What do you think?"

"Pure pirate!" cried Patrick. "They're brilliant!" And he was so happy he threw his three-cornered hat in the air. Then Henrietta jumped on to his shoulder and they both danced on the deck and sang their favourite pirate song.

"Yo, ho, ho and a bottle of rum!"

WIZARD

Caroline Pitcher

"Look, Wizard," cried Laura, pointing to a sticker in a car window. *"A dog is for life, not just for Christmas."*

Wizard wagged his tail. *A dog is for life …* and there it was again, that word, *Criss-muss.*

Laura, Rob and Dad were on their way back from taking Wizard for a lovely long walk in the woods. They had taken it in turns to throw a ball for him to chase among the trees.

When they got home, Wizard smelled another tree. In the corner of the living room there was a tall pine tree in a pot.

Laura and Rob clapped and cheered. The children began to decorate the tree with shiny things. They hung coloured glittery balls on the ends of the branches.

"Don't chase these balls, Wizard," said Laura.

Wizard watched as she stood on a chair and fixed a silver shape on top of the tree. It was like the sparkles Wizard saw in the sky at night.

"Hey, Wizard. Here is your first Christmas tree and this is the Christmas star!" said Laura. "It showed the three kings where the baby was. The star

helps people to
find things."

Wizard
wagged his
tail, which
was feathery
and almost as
long as he
was. He
was small
and black

with ginger eyebrows shaped like little
boomerangs. The top of his head was
pointed. When the family first saw him at the
Dog Rescue Home, Rob said, "That puppy is
a mixture of everything. He's a mutt. And his
head is pointy like a wizard's hat."

So that was how Wizard got his name.

The family chose him out of all the dogs. He went to live with Laura, Rob, Mum and Dad and everything was wonderful.

But everything was about to change...

"We've finished decorating," shouted Laura. "Bring on the presents!"

Mum brought packages in bright paper and put them under the tree. There was a smell Wizard didn't like in some of the presents, all flowery and perfumed like the bathroom. *Pooh!* But he could smell chocolate in others...

Laura put a last present under the tree. "That's for you, Wizard," she whispered. "Don't open it until Christmas Day."

Wizard had a good sniff at the present.

It smelled of the pet shop – a mix of biscuits, plastic toys, fish food, rabbits and budgerigars. He put his paw on it. It squeaked and Wizard jumped.

Mum laughed. "Dad's got another present on the way, for all of us," she said. "I hope you'll like it too, Wizard." She put her finger to her lips. *Shhhh!*

On Christmas Eve, Wizard did not sleep very well. He was too excited, and there was a different scent in the house. Wizard thought he knew what it was, but he couldn't be sure. It smelled like one of those creatures he sometimes saw when he was out for walks. The ones that hissed and spat. The ones he wanted to chase, but Laura always said he couldn't.

Christmas morning was all paper-tearing and chocolate-eating. Laura gave Wizard his present straight away. He held it down with his paw and ripped back the paper with his teeth. Inside was a toy chicken with a squeaky tummy. *Wow!* Wizard soon got busy, and nobody told him off when he tore his chicken and pulled out all the stuffing and the squeaker from inside. *Great!* Wizard wagged his tail so hard it swept Mum's glass off the table. "Lucky it's empty," she said.

"Now time for the SURPRISE PRESENT!" said Dad. He hurried out and Mum held Wizard by the collar. Dad came back holding a cardboard pet carrier with a pink bow around it. He set the carrier down on the floor.

A furry face was peeping through the little window.

Wizard heard a tiny mew.

Dad opened the top and out jumped a silver kitten.

Wizard's heart sank.

"Ooooh! Aw! Isn't she cute!" shrieked Rob, picking up the wriggling kitten. "What shall we call her?"

"How about *Purr*fect? She looks so beautiful," cried Laura, hopping up and down, impatient for her turn.

Wizard wondered why they were bothering to choose a name. Cats didn't care what name you gave them. They didn't come when you called them. Not like dogs.

In the end, they could not decide what to call her, so she was just Kitten for now. She was pretty (as kittens go), with fluffy silver fur and green eyes. "Look at her whiskers," breathed Laura. "They're like gossamer. They kind of twinkle…"

Kitten was cuddled on knees all morning. She was only put down on the floor when it was time for lunch. When she yawned, her eyes grew even bigger and her open mouth was bubblegum pink, with ridges on the top and sharp little teeth. She curled up among the cushions on the sofa like a furry Catherine wheel.

When Wizard tried to jump up on the sofa and sit there too, Dad said, "Wizard, you know you're not allowed on the furniture."

Wizard had to sleep in his dog basket in the kitchen.

Kitten got presents every day, even after they took the tree away. She had a special spoon for her food with a smiling cat face on the handle and her own dish with paw prints around the rim. Her tins were full of bright pink goo, but Wizard was not allowed to eat any.

Mum cooked fish for Kitten. Wizard licked his lips but Mum said, "Dogs don't eat fish." *But they'd like to try some...* thought Wizard.

"You're so furry," murmured Laura, stroking the kitten on her knee. "Furry … fairy … maybe we should call her Tinkerbell? Or Twinkerbell?"

The family said yes. So Kitten became Twinkerbell, or Twinks for short.

"Now you both have magic names," said Laura. "I'm sure the two of you will be the best of friends."

Wizard wasn't so sure…

The children bought Twinkerbell a floppy frog full of rice and a toy mouse stuffed with catnip, but she preferred chasing leaves and spiders. Most of all, she couldn't resist Wizard's tail! She pounced on it every time it wagged. Her claws were sharp and they hurt.

At least Twinkerbell wasn't allowed out into the garden yet. Wizard was! He loved the garden, especially at night. He loved the silver sparkles high in the sky. They stayed in one place. Not like planes. Wizard barked at planes. They zoomed over his garden, so he barked to scare them away.

But one afternoon the kitten *was* allowed out. Rob and Laura put on their coats and carried her into the garden. Wizard went too.

"Fetch!" cried Rob and threw his ball. Wizard chased it and fetched it back to Rob. Twinkerbell looked shocked as if to say, "Why would anyone want to do anything as silly as that?" She pounced on an old leaf instead. Wizard pounced too, he couldn't help it, he just wanted to play, but the kitten scampered off and disappeared. Wizard ran around the garden, nose down to her scent. Where was she?

Something touched Wizard's back. It dabbed and dabbed again. He spun round and saw Twinkerbell hanging upside down from the branch at the bottom of a tree, swiping his tail with her paw as if she was fishing. Wizard leaped up at the tree trunk, barking.

It was no good. That was when Wizard found out that cats can climb trees and dogs cannot.

The postman made matters worse. Wizard did not like the postman, because he came right up to the house and rattled the letter box. One morning he rang the bell. Mum picked up Twinkerbell and went to answer the door, and Wizard went to protect Mum. When the postman saw Twinkerbell, he went all gooey and drooled, "Aw! So sweet! What kind of cat is that? Must have cost a lot! Is it a pedigree?"

Wizard did not know what a pedigree was. It sounded smart. No one *ever* asked, "What kind of dog is that?" No one thought *he* was a "pedigree", whatever that was.

Wizard loved his family as much as ever, and he was still warm and walked and fed and patted. But it wasn't the same as having them all to himself. And everywhere he was, the kitten seemed to be too. Every time he curled up for a sleep, Twinkerbell pounced on his tail or dabbed his nose. Once he even found her dozing in his dog basket.

Twinkerbell could bat him with her paw full of tiny claws and the family all laughed. If he gave a warning growl, they said, "Oh, no, no, Wizard! You'll scare her. She's only a little kitten."

Then Mum came back from the pet shop with a little door called a cat-flap.

"So Twinks can let herself in and out on her own," she said.

What about a dog-flap? Wizard had to bark for someone to open the back door if he wanted to go outside.

That day, Laura and Rob brought friends home after school. They patted Wizard, but then they went out into the garden to play with Twinkerbell, teasing her with a ball of wool. Wizard slunk off to his basket.

The children played outside with Twinkerbell until Mum called them in for tea. They coaxed Twinkerbell in through her little door, worse luck.

After tea the visitors went home. Mum asked, "Where is Twinks? It's time for her dinner."

Wizard had his nose down in his own bowl, snaffling up his biscuits. He heard the children calling, "Twinkerbell? Twinks!" all around the house. He hoped Mum would put the kitten's dish down so that he could clean it up for her, but she didn't.

The children went on searching, under beds, in the cupboard beneath the stairs, the cloakroom, even in the empty washing machine. No Twinkerbell.

When Dad came home from work, Laura ran up to him. "We've lost her. We've lost Twinkerbell! She must have gone out through her catflap," she wailed, then she burst into tears. Wizard couldn't bear to hear her crying. He began to whimper.

"Don't worry," Dad said. "She'll be hiding somewhere."

The family searched the house. No luck. Wizard crept to his bed. He wished that kitten would come back — he hated his family being unhappy.

As usual, after his dinner, Wizard wanted to go in the garden. Without a word, Laura let him outside. It was dark now and there were sparkles in the sky. Wizard gazed up at them.

There was one very big sparkle, like that silver shape Laura had put at the top of the Christmas tree. It stayed in the sky as if it was frozen, high above the tall tree. As if it was showing him something...

Wizard heard a noise. He saw a dark

shape near the top of the tree.

Wizard stared. The shape wriggled.

"Mee-ow ... mee-ow?" The noise was sad and plaintive. It was Twinks!

This must be a game! thought Wizard. *Come on down, Kitten!* he barked.

But she didn't. She mewed again. Then Wizard realized that she couldn't come down. She was well and truly stuck. He turned tail and raced back to the house, barking and barking and leaping up at Laura.

"Be quiet, Wizard!" ordered Dad.

But Laura said, "I think Wizard is trying to tell us something."

Wizard turned tail and ran to the door again, barking furiously, and at last they followed him into the garden.

Wizard stopped in front of the tree with the star above it. There was the faint sound of mewing.

"It's Twinkerbell!" cried Laura.

"Get a torch, Dad, and a ladder," shouted Rob. Dad was no good at heights so Mum went up the ladder instead and brought Twinkerbell safely down.

"Clever Wizard!" cried Laura, throwing her arms around his neck. "You're the best dog ever!"

"Wizard, you truly are a Magic Mutt," said Rob. Mum gave Wizard special Streaky Dog Treats, and in the morning Dad took him for an extra long walk in the fields.

Now when Twinkerbell pads up to play with Wizard, she no longer has her claws out and she doesn't pounce painfully on his tail. She cuddles up to him and purrs. And Wizard no longer minds Twinkerbell sleeping in his basket. Once Wizard got used to her, it was cosy company, and warm on cold winter nights.

Now that Wizard shares his home with Laura, Rob, Mum and Dad – and Twinkerbell, his tail wags more than ever.

PRINCESS MIA AND THE MOONBEAR

Malachy Doyle

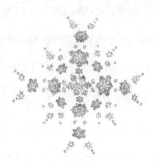

Mia was a wild child, with sea-green eyes and hair as black as midnight. She lived with her father in the land of snow and ice, and there was nothing she liked more than to wander near and far, talking to the birds and animals.

Winters are hard in the frozen north and the cold slips its icy fingers into your bones, no matter how well you wrap up. People have to go outside at least once a day, to fetch water from holes they've made in the ice, but after they've done that they hurry back into the warmth of their homes and they stay there.

Unless you're a princess, that is. If you're a princess, living in a palace made of ice that never melts, then someone fetches your water for you and everything else you need, so you don't have to go outside at all. Which would be fine if you're the sort of person who likes having everything done for you, but it wasn't all right for Mia.

"PLEASE let me go out, Father!" she begged the king. She'd been asking for days, but this time she wasn't going to accept no for an answer. She'd thrown on every single one of her furs, so there was no way he could say she'd be too cold. "I'm so bored with being indoors!" she cried. "I've read every book there is to read, played every game there is to play and I'm bored, bored, BORED!"

"Oh, Mia." The king sighed. "All you ever want to do is to run wild. You'll have to settle down before you marry, you know."

"I'm NEVER going to marry!" vowed the princess. "No one's EVER going to tame me! Please, Father … please let me go out," she begged. "Just for a while."

"Oh, very well," said the king, who was nearly as fed up with saying no as his daughter was with hearing it. "But don't stay out too long. And remember to watch out for bears."

Mia did as her father said, but not in the way he meant. She ran to the mouth of the cave where she knew the polar bears were sleeping and she sang a little song, over and over until they woke.

One by one, the bears clambered out to see if it was springtime. It didn't take them long to realize that it was still the middle of winter, but they were happy to see their friend Mia again, for she'd been coming to visit them for years.

"Aninga!" cried the princess, when she spotted one in particular. Rushing over to him, she threw her arms around his neck and gave him a big bear hug. For Aninga was her favourite, and they'd been playing together since he was just a cub.

She climbed up on to the polar bear's back and he raced with her up and down the hillside, before tipping her, giggling, into a great pile of snow.

That was the way of it, every winter, until the king decided that it was time for Mia to find a husband. People marry young, so young, in the frozen north and many hunters came to the ice palace, hoping to win her hand. They brought all sorts of gifts – one offered her whalebone, another brought sealskins, and a third some pretty little animals that he'd carved from the tusk of a walrus.

Sometimes Mia accepted one of their gifts, if she particularly liked it, but as for the men...

"Oh, Father," she complained, "I can't spend more than five minutes with any one of them. They're all so BORING!"

And she flew outside to run with the bears, who were so much wilder, so much more exciting, so much more fun than any man.

It was midwinter's night, and someone came knocking on Princess Mia's window. She went over to see who it was and, by the light of her candle, saw a stranger, with his hood drawn tight around his face.

"Who are you?" she said. "What do you want?" But there was no answer. "If you're one of those annoying young men who want to marry me, you can go back where you came from," she told him. "I've had enough of you all!"

The stranger turned away, but Mia stayed by the window. The full moon shone on to the snow and she wanted, more than anything, to be out there, dancing in the beautiful midwinter light. She knew her father wouldn't like her to, though, so she returned to her bed, pulling the blankets up tight around her.

She tossed and she turned, she turned and she tossed and, after about an hour, went back over to the window. The stranger was still there outside, now asleep in the snow.

"He must be freezing!" she said to herself. "I wonder who he is and why he didn't go away, like I told him to." And she decided to go and find out.

Wrapping herself up all cosy-warm in her bedding, she tiptoed from her room, down the narrow staircase, and out into the snow. Creeping up to the stranger and peeping in under his hood, she was most surprised to see a shiny black nose.

She had a feeling that she knew who it was then, so she tickled the nose, and the stranger opened two dark little eyes, with the flames of a fire glinting inside.

"Aninga!" cried Mia, for that is who it was – her very special, life-long friend. "You've come to do a midwinter moondance with me! You've come to be my Moonbear!"

Pulling him to his feet, she did a twirly-whirly dance with him, skipping and laughing in the moonlight, before climbing up on to his back. She clung on tightly, as Aninga galloped off into the snow, and after a while the warmth of her Moonbear sent her into a deep, deep sleep.

Princess Mia woke to find herself in a cave, all lined with fur and feathers. It was Aninga's cave, she guessed, but there was no sign of him. *He's probably gone off to find some fish for our breakfast*, she thought, and settled down to wait.

After a while, though, she heard a noise from outside the cave, and it didn't sound like bears. Creeping to the opening, Mia spied two hunters coming towards her across the snow.

Fear ran through her then, for she knew these two. Both had asked her to marry them and both had been angry when she'd turned them down. "Oh why is Aninga not here?" she muttered. But then she heard a roar from the far side of the hill. "He's back!" she gasped.

Mia watched as her Moonbear bounded towards the hunters. One of them threw down his weapon and ran off, but the other stood his ground. It wasn't her the hunter had come to harm, the princess realized, but Aninga himself!

The bear rushed towards him but the

cruel hunter, waiting until he was near enough, hurled his spear, and Aninga fell.

"No!" Mia rushed to his side. She cradled her Moonbear's head in her arms, but the fire in his eyes was fading.

The hunter, watching from a distance, slipped away when he saw all the other bears come out from their caves to form a circle around Aninga.

"Don't leave me, Moonbear!" cried Mia, weeping over her friend. "Please don't leave me!"

Her tears fell on his body and as they did, something magical happened. Aninga's eyes re-opened, and to the princess it was like she was looking at herself, reflected deep inside him. She realized, then, that his coal-black eyes had turned emerald green, like hers. And that he was changing – strangely changing.

His legs were becoming arms. His paws were becoming hands. His face … his face…

"A man!" cried Mia, her own eyes wide in wonder. "You're becoming a man!"

"A prince, actually – Prince Aninga," he said, smiling up at her. There was a bear-like growl to his voice, but he was human, definitely human.

She looked deep into his eyes, though, to check if it was still her Moonbear in another form. And there were the flames of his wildness, sparkling inside.

"Yes!" Mia laughed. "You really are my Prince Aninga!"

Taking him by the hand, she pulled him to his feet. And they danced together in the midwinter snow, Princess Mia and Prince Aninga – the wild child and the Moonbear.

WOLF MOON

Elizabeth Baguley

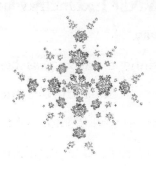

"I'll go," said Elgiva. Her mother lay pale in her bed. The baby was taking such a long time to be born and someone had to fetch Elgiva's aunt, who knew how to bring children into the world. Father needed to stay and help in the best way he could. Young as she was, Elgiva wanted to help too. Father hugged her close. "You're a good girl," he said, as he helped her on with her woollen cloak. He lit the lantern from the fire and gave it to her to light her way.

Elgiva slung a bag across her shoulder, packed with bread and cold meat for the journey, then opened the door of the hut. The forest pressed close, thick liquid night filling up the space between every trunk and branch. Through all this gloom and across the bitter snow she must go alone. Always before she had gone with her mother. Always before they had travelled in the daytime when the wolves did not hunt. But however afraid she was, Mother needed her to fetch help and Elgiva would not let her down.

It was so dark! Elgiva had to find the path which would take her by Whispering Hollow and on through the forest to her aunt's house. But the path was just a thread through the trees where the snow had been trodden by other travellers and was not easy to make out. She looked up through the winter-bare branches and searched the sky for the moon, hoping that its light would help her to find her way. Where yesterday its thin curve had cut a slice of light through the sky, now there was nothing.

"It's the time of the Wolf Moon," she said aloud, her voice croaky with alarm. She remembered the story that her mother had told her since she was small – that at midwinter, if the snow lay on the ground and there was no food for the wolves and they were hungry, they would steal the moon. Only if all the villagers said their prayers would it come back, small and shivering from the terror it had suffered while the wolves had kept it. The time of the Wolf Moon was a time of the deepest darkness and the greatest danger.

Elgiva whispered a prayer under her breath, a prayer to keep her safe from the wolves. She could hear them now, their cries like a cruel song. She imagined them, moving together through the darkness in their pack, weaving amongst each other, so many of them. She imagined what it would be like to feel their rough fur around her legs and see the ice-flash of their teeth.

"But they're far away," she whispered to herself. Although she could hear their cry, it was faint as a ghost, so she was safe – at least for the moment. The prayer felt warm inside her and the lantern made a small halo of light so that she could just make out the path writing a line in the snow. She felt hopeful as she trod it, sure that she would bring back her aunt so that all would be well.

After a while, the path began to slope down towards Whispering Hollow. It was not far to her aunt's now. Although her legs were tired and the branches caught at her clothes and hair, Elgiva was pleased with the speed she was making. A dream came colourful into her head. She saw herself returning home with Aunt Edith, who would bring soothing herbs and a kind voice to her mother. The baby would be born safely, and Father would hold it in his big, gentle bear-grip. Mother would smile and stroke Elgiva's hair and ask about her brave journey. She could almost feel the softness of her mother's hands, holding her tight and safe.

Suddenly, the dream was snatched away. Elgiva was tripping, slipping, falling. The dark sky and the icy earth were tossing her between them as she crashed down the steep hill.

At last she stopped, and for a while she did not move. When she did, a cry tore from her lips. Her ankle had twisted beneath her and would not take her weight.

Worse still, the lantern had fallen from her hand and she was in complete darkness. Shocked and dizzy, she couldn't seem to think where she was or what she was doing.

"Mother!" she called out. Then the world flooded back, black and icy and wild. Mother was far away and now here she was, lying injured in the forest on the night of the Wolf Moon.

"But I won't let you down, Mother," she gasped, rubbing her ankle hard and screwing up her eyes so that the tears would not fall.

If I can crawl a little, she thought, *I can find a stick to lean on and then I'll be able to walk.*

She saw that she had rolled away from the path in her fall and now she was at the bottom of Whispering Hollow. Brambles clawed at her and however hard she strained her eyes, in the deeper darkness here, the path stayed hidden. Things could not be worse – could they?

As Elgiva crawled carefully along, feeling amongst the frozen leaves and stones for a strong stick to help her to her feet, a twist of snow began to spiral into the hollow. It was blowing in coils that wound about her like a cold snake. It settled on the ground to hide every sign of the path. Now, Elgiva knew what it was to be truly, utterly, completely, deeply alone.

Or perhaps she wasn't. From nearby came the sounds of a creature stirring and coming towards her. Twigs cracked, sticks shifted. Terrified, Elgiva pulled herself up against a tree trunk. She wanted to run but could only freeze, waiting to see what would appear.

The snow curtain drew back and Elgiva saw a wolf, small and young, hardly more than a cub. Seeing the girl it stopped, one paw raised. Its fur was snow-white, its teeth ice-white. Some glint of elf-light caught its eyes and they seemed to have no colour.

Elgiva's heart pounded. Small though it was, it would still be powerful and at midwinter when the snow was on the ground, it would be hungry. How could she escape?

Elgiva dropped swiftly to her knees, grasped a heavy, rounded stone, drew her hand behind her head in aim – but then stopped. Away, away in the far distance, the pack called and the wolf, turning an ear, whimpered. Elgiva heard the sound and understood how it must feel.

Beneath the thick pelt, the wolf's shoulders were bony. It looked so thin and hungry that perhaps it had been too weak to keep up with the pack. Like Elgiva it was away from its kind and lost. Far off, a she-wolf howled, and the cub whimpered back, its small voice muffled by the snow, trying to call its mother.

Instead of throwing the stone, Elgiva placed it on the ground. Then she lowered her eyes as her father had taught her to do if an angry dog threatened her and shuffled backwards, away from the wolf. Carefully, she reached into her bag and brought out her chunk of meat. She pushed the food forward to lie next to the dropped stone. Then she waited.

The small wolf sniffed and delicately edged towards the food. Unable to help itself, it snatched up the meat and began to chew. All this while, Elgiva was a statue. By now her ankle hurt less and her head was clear. *I have only to wait and the wolf will go*, she told herself. Then, if she could find the path in the darkness, she might still reach her aunt's house. If only she could *see*.

But the wolf did not go. It licked its lips and came towards Elgiva – but this time as it looked at her, she looked it in the eye. The wolf was not attacking her – it moved too slowly for that. It was picking something up from the ground in its jaws and carrying it towards Elgiva before dropping it at her feet – a gift.

It was the stone which the girl had thought of throwing. The small wolf sat on its haunches. Elgiva took up the stone once again, expecting to feel its weight fill her palm. Instead it was light as a handful of snow, so light that it began to float, rising upwards. Now it began to gleam, then glow. Up through the trees it rose, pulling behind it a swirl of frost-sparkling snow like angel-hair. Finally it came to rest, round and full, spilling light across the forest.

"You gave us back the Wolf-Moon," gasped Elgiva to the small wolf, but it listened only to its mother's voice which cut through the forest. Strengthened by the meat, the small wolf howled back. Completely unafraid now, Elgiva looked into its clear eyes as it looked full at her for a moment before setting off to find its mother. Elgiva knew that she, too, must continue on her journey.

In the soft moonlight, the path was clear to see and although her ankle still hurt, Elgiva made good time as she followed it. Before long, she was with her aunt and they were crossing back through the forest, hoping that they would be in time to help. As they reached the hut, Elgiva's father opened the door. "You have come too late," he said, his voice gruff.

Too late! Was the baby safe? Had something happened to her mother? And now, Elgiva wept. She had tried so hard and still she had failed in her errand.

But her father's voice was gruff with smiles, not tears. For inside the hut, her mother lay in the bed exactly where Elgiva had left her, but in her arms a tiny baby, its sleeping face lit through the window by the light of the wolf-given moon.